Spring Things

by **Bob Raczka**

illustrated by **Judy Stead**

JR
P

Albert Whitman & Company
Morton Grove, Illinois

Library of Congress Cataloging-in-Publication Data

Raczka, Bob.
Spring things / by Bob Raczka ; illustrated by Judy Stead.
p. cm.
Summary: Winter melts into spring with the sights and sounds of hopping and skipping,
sowing and mowing, and blading and lemonading.
ISBN 13: 978-0-8075-7596-3 (hardcover)
1. Spring—Fiction. 2. Stories in rhyme. [1. Nature—Fiction.] I. Stead, Judy, ill. II. Title.
PZ8.3.R11153Spr 2007 [E]—dc22 2006023403

The book is set in Minion Pro and Dandelion.
The design is by Carol Gildar.

For more information about Albert Whitman & Company,
please visit our web site at www.albertwhitman.com.

To Emma, my Honey Bunny, who was born in the spring. —B.R.

For Zoe and Nick, and for James, with special thanks. —J.S.

Melting,

dripping,

cold's grip slipping.

Sunning, warming,

thunderstorming.

Budding,

sprouting,

trees leaf-outing.

Throwing,

catching,

babies hatching.

Hopping,

skipping,

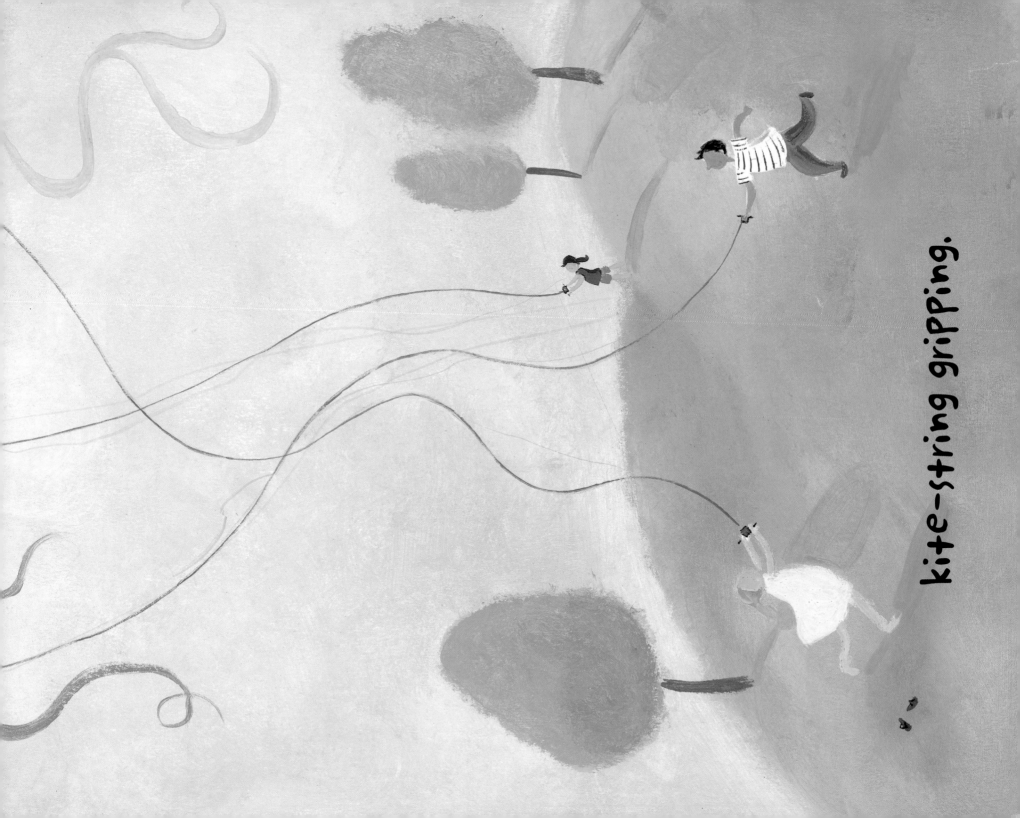

kite-string gripping.

Biking, blading,

lemonading.

Hoeing,

sowing,

mowers mowing.

Buzzing, humming—

summer's coming!

Spring.

One Last Thing . . .

Earth has seasons, four in all—
winter, spring, summer, fall.

Here's a little seasons quiz:
(I'll bet you're a seasons whiz!).

1. Spring means sun and thundershowers,
   planting seeds and growing _ _ _ _ _ _ _.

2. Summer means time out from school,
   ice cream cones and swimming _ _ _ _ _.

3. Fall means apple pies to bake,
   corn to pick and leaves to _ _ _ _.

4. Winter means the north winds blow,
   the air turns cold and clouds bring _ _ _ _.

Winter, spring, summer, fall—
which do *you* love best of all?

1. flowers 2. pools 3. rake 4. snow